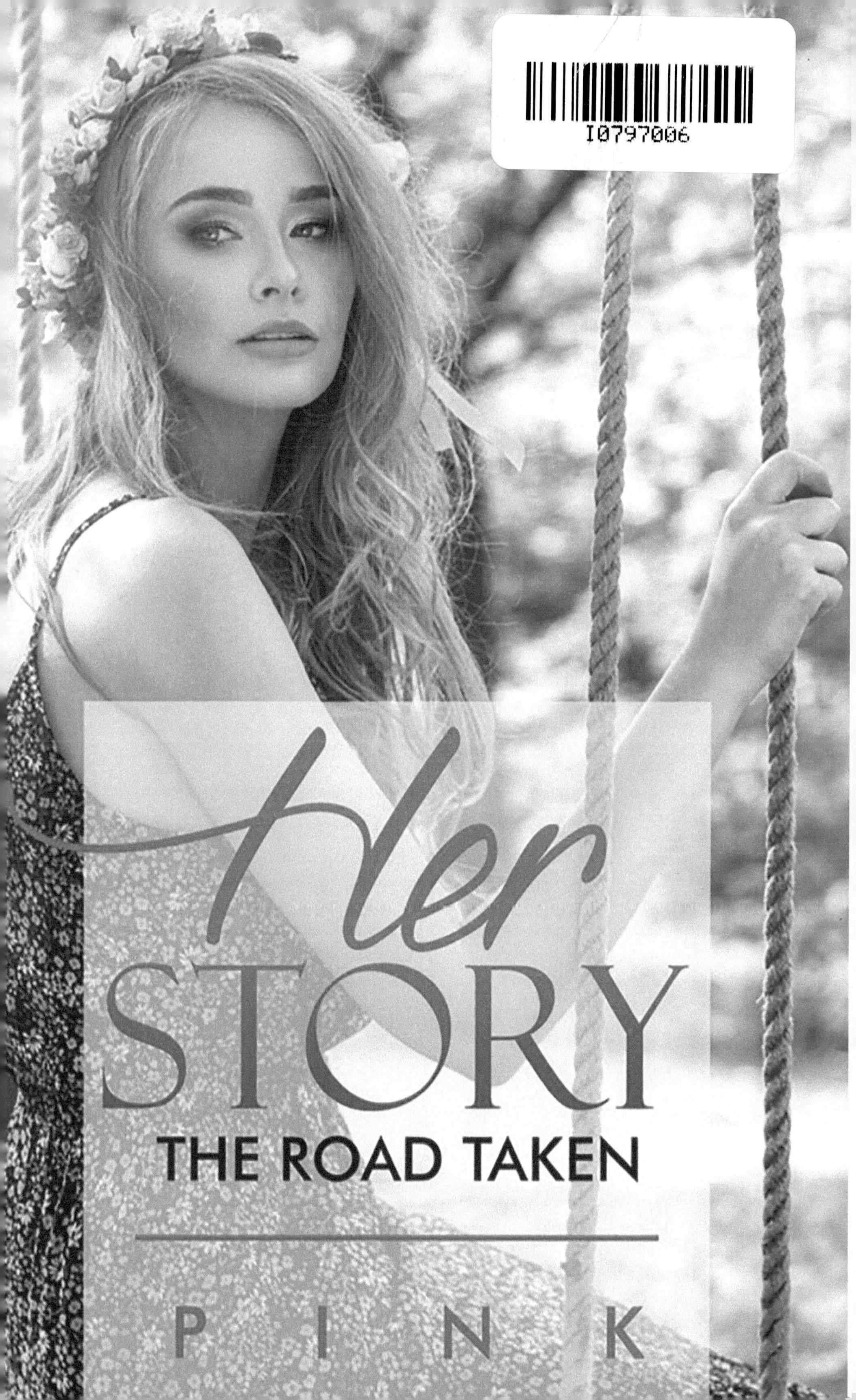
I0797006
Her
STORY
THE ROAD TAKEN
P I N K

# Pink says Hi!

# Her Story

# Her Story

## The Road Taken

**Pink**

**ARPress**
45 Dan Rd., Suite 36
Canton MA 02021
Hotline: 1(800) 220-7660
Fax: 1(855) 752-6001

Ordering Information:

Quantity sales. Special discounts are available on quantity purchases by corporations, associations, and others. For details, contact the publisher at the address above.

Printed in the United States of America.
Library of Congress Control Number

| ISBN-13: | Paperback | 979-8-89389-055-6 |
|---|---|---|
| | ePub | 979-8-89389-056-3 |

Rev. date: 03/20/2019

This is a story of a young girl who had a baby out of wedlock.
And the story of the baby's life.

This is an old man saying . . .
If a man can get the milk for free, why buy the cow.

The Sinner's Prayer

Ask Jesus Christ to come into your heart,
Ask Jesus Christ to pardon your sin nature,
be sorry for your sins.
Ask Jesus Christ to keep your name safe in the
Lamb's Book of Life.

. . . Amen.

Her name is Bonnie Booker, and outside this dank cabin, endless flakes of snow flurried and then fell to the ground or stuck to the windows as time slowly ticked out the destiny that she was not aware that she had chosen. She could not even have dreamt the path her life would take. Each moment created a thread in the tapestry of life that would remain indelible for all time.

Bonnie's father was John Conway's foreman, and her family lived on his land. It was early spring of 1863, and Bonnie knew that she did not like to be poor.

The winds made whirring sounds way into the night. The gales caused her to shudder as she tried to light a fire in a dusty brick fireplace and put on a kettle of water on the grate. The wind blew the fire out, but she persisted to bend over the hearth re-lighting it and watching it smolder into the blackened wood. The fire moved as if it were slowly writing on the wood making swirling designs and then fading into a faint stream of charcoal and smoke.

She went to the mirror and washed her face. Her hair was flaxen nearly platinum blonde, and her eyes were medium violet blue. She was the oldest daughter in her family. There were nine children.

All of her dreams, she thought, hinged on the man who was coming. She was poor, and he was wealthy.

A large horse and buggy slowly straddled the winding dirt road and came to a stop beside the cabin, and out jumped a middle-aged man. He had a bristled mustache and beard. His dark brown suit was ordered from a store up North. It had a satin lining, trousers and matching vest with a pocket on each side for a watch and chain.

"How are you, Miss Bonnie?" The man asked. "Sorry I haven't been able to see you for several weeks, but I have been busy with the cattle this time of year. They're so susceptible to disease or either they're calving, and Miss Nettie hasn't been feeling well."

Bonnie thought who cares about Nettie or the cows getting sick. She could only think about her own expectations and her own problems, for she was pregnant.

"I'm pregnant," Bonnie said.

"I know that, and I'm sorry for you, girl."

John Conway's face broke out into a big grin. "Guess I'll have to fire your daddy so all of you will leave here."

"You would fire Daddy?" Bonnie cried.

"Nettie is near to having a baby herself, she's my wife. I don't want her to be hurt; she's been a good wife and takes good care of me."

"But, aren't you going to help me? Don't I mean anything to you?"

"Not really," John grunted. "I just came to tell you goodbye."

"Goodbye," he said, lifting his hat and pulling on his mustache. He made a little bow, his back already bowed over as if he had sat over accounting books for years and years. The door shut, letting in a freezing wind, as a thousand beautiful dreams flew out the window.

Bonnie was fifteen years old and was a stranger to books. She was not a good housekeeper and liked to dream lying in the grass in the warm sunlight.

Laying aside the fact that John was married, Bonnie was no match for Nettie. Nettie was a well-organized, spotless housekeeper. The child Nettie was carrying was her fifth, and except for John's misbehaving from time to time, the Conway household was as solid as granite.

Spring had come, Nettie had a son. The countryside seemed at peace. Spring planting had come and gone, summer and early autumn with its cool air and warm sun contrasted in the bright yellow hay and cold gray shadows as the sun went down. It was September; Bonnie was nearing the time when she would have her baby.

The day she had a little girl, father said that after a short time that she would have to give the baby up. The baby was given the name Lilly.

Lilly was a good baby, not like the rest of the Booker family. She showed a unique intelligence from her earliest beginnings. She looked a little like her mother, but much more like her father. Her demeanor and the way that she projected herself was much more identifiable with the Conway family. This amused Bonnie as she was set on keeping Lilly.

Her father had long since lost his job with Mr. Conway. He was very bitter not having the well-paying job he had lost. He swore to himself that he would get even, and nothing Bonnie's mother could say could persuade him to alter his plan.

When Lilly was weaned and walking, Tom Booker took her into town when Bonnie was out berry picking. She had left Lilly with her mother who had wanted to give Bonnie some time to herself. Tom Booker took this opportunity to take the child by force and rode into town with Lilly in his wagon.

He rode up to John Conway' s General Store, tied the reins to the hitching post, he took the child (under his arm) like a croaker sack full of potatoes and placed her up on the counter. As he did this, John came out of his office. There were some twelve to fifteen people in the store buying goods.

Tom Booker shouted, "Be sure your sins will find you out!" He steadied Lilly on the counter and left. She began to cry pitifully and started to teeter backward, then forwards, but John Conway caught her by her arm just in time.

No one made a sound, but one could tell plenty of gossips would be going around for many months, maybe years.

John decided to take the child home and make a full confession to Nettie, Lilly was wet and very hungry when they got to the house.

"I don't want her here, John, it's not good for me, and it's not good for the children."

"But she's my child too, dear. Please keep her. Let her help you around the house. Raise her as you want to. I won't say a word."

"All right, if I can have complete control of her, we'll keep her."

A year passed and then two years, and Lilly was being brutally treated. No one stopped Nettie from making bruise marks all over Lilly's body. Even John winced, as she squeezed Lilly's cheeks together, he heard her say, "You shut up young lady do you hear me?" "You shut up!" But John said nothing at the ill-treatment that Nettie was giving Lilly.

Bonnie could not forgive her father for taking Lilly from her. As the following third spring turned into summer, she began to gather up the courage to go and get her child.

She began to walk miles and miles; it did not seem to faze her. Obstacles would not keep her from her mission. The past began to come to her mind. When she lay with John and the promises he never kept. Her destiny seemed to be going on a downward spiral.

Tears rimmed the lids of her eyes as she entered the Conway farmland. She saw Lilly helping Nettie beating rugs. Lilly would give her the batting stick if she dropped it. Bonnie approached Nettie.

"Ma'am, I want my Lilly back. That's all I want, and then I'll be going."

"Girl," Nettie retorted, "I'm keeping her as my help."

"I'm not going till I have my Lilly, Mrs. Conway."

With one blow of the batting stick, Nettie hit Bonnie on the back. Bonnie fought her as hard as she could, but Nettie hit her again and again with the stick. Bonnie sank to the ground. Two men came to help Bonnie when they saw what was happening.

"Get her off my property and away from my house and my belongings. I don't want to see her again!" Nettie shouted.

The two men carried Bonnie away.

"And don't come back!" Nettie shouted again.

With this last try to retrieve her daughter, Bonnie reluctantly gave up, for she knew the Conway family was too strong for her. She walked in a very bright light for a little while, then disappeared in the thick green woods like a gray brown deer.

Now Lilly Conway grew. She was nearly three years old when John Conway steadied her on the counter in his General Store. He had no love for her and felt no duty to Bonnie Booker. Yet, Lilly was part of him, and so he took her into his home as his daughter. But Nettie did not see her as a daughter. She was more like an intruder. There was no room in Nettie's heart for her husband's bastard child. How could he force this child on her when she had born him a son? Without really realizing it, Nettie subconsciously began a plan of cold revenge. It grew as the years passed by with little subsiding as if from one crescendo to the next. The beatings and bruises were set in the woods beyond the house.

The crying sounded like a cat crying from a distance.

It was on just one of these occasions that Esther, Lilly's half sister, did not go to school and found her mother beating Lilly.

"Mother, why are you doing this?"

Lilly was four and a half years old and Esther was nine.

"I'm going to make a good girl out of this whelp. She'll do just what I say. She won't have a lazy bone in her when I get through with her."

Lilly was crying hysterically and threw up some oatmeal on some dried leaves that had settled for several weeks.

"Let me take Lilly," said Esther. "I'll take her back to the house and give her some milk. I want some milk too, Mama."

Mrs. Conway grabbed the blackberries she and Lilly had been picking and went down a narrow path to find another patch. Esther gently took Lilly by the hand and walked down the path toward the house. The milk and fried peach pies sure tasted good after the traumatic scene in the woods. Lilly looked up and smiled at Esther as she slowly savored her pie. After that, Esther listened intently for any more cries out in the woods or in the house, for she had grown to love her half-sister very much. This was the beginning of a change in Lilly's life. A sweetness that she had never known emitted from her sister.

Mrs. Conway could not discipline Lilly severely when Esther was near. And Esther would play school teacher and would try to teach Lilly what she learned that day in school. Out of an awesome tragedy loomed a pretty happy childhood except Nettie would look for chances to take Lilly into the woods and to work her unceasingly, until she would drop into bed at night. John Conway would look upon all proceedings in his household with little reflection. His main interests were the General Store, the grist mill, the farm, and the education of his only truly daughter, Esther Conway. The whole family loved her very much. She could write and draw so John decided to send her away to an art school in New York. This made Lilly very much afraid because she would be left alone with Nettie again. Her fear was so prolific that she became ill for several weeks. Esther left for New York the last of spring. She studied at the New York School of Commercial Art for a year.

In Citrus on a Friday night, all the young people congregated in the town square. After working hard all week, the youth of Citrus were interested in any gossip, what new clothes were being worn by whom, and who was going with who, or who was going to be married and when. It was a sacred courting ground, and many young people who had promenaded it perimeters found themselves winding up at a church altar or a Justice of Peace. But that's not where Lilly met Bart.

It was a long walk to the mailbox that was stationed at the front of the Conway farm. Lilly watched the big grandfather clock for the hands to strike 11 :30 A.M. A new postman had been delivering mail for several weeks, and it was one of Lilly's jobs to fetch the mail. It was hard for her not to show delight when Nettie told her to fetch the mail; for Lilly was highly interested in Bart Hadley. Though she was fifteen, and he was twenty-five meant nothing to her. The difference was only in numbers. So, when it was time for him to deliver the mail, she had a pitcher of sweet lemonade, sandwiches and tea cakes wrapped and put in a large basket. Bart Hadley and Lilly actually started dating in front of the Conway mailbox. She was very young and yet could hardly wait until she would start raising a family of her own.

"Lilly, you're just a baby," Bart would say.

"I am not I can do anything any other woman can do. I'm just as much a woman as anybody in town."

"Well, I guess you are," said Bart. "You sure can cook. These cakes are real tasty. Got any more? Yes sir, you sure can cook. I know a pretty glen near the backwaters. Why don't I take you there after church and we'll have a picnic? It's a nice drive and we'll get home plenty before dark."

"I'll have to ask my mama first," Lilly said, looking down.

"She may want me to help her with dinner."

When the last little bit of lemonade was swilled down, Bart went on the rest of his rounds, and Lilly walked back to the house. She felt very sad because she knew that Mrs. Conway would never let her date Bart, even though his father owned a general store on the other side of town like her father's. She would never want her it to marry that well. So, when she asked her, she knew beforehand what the verdict would be.

"Oh! No! You don't young lady; you have chores to do here. That man is ten years older than you, and his family is steeped in tradition and high society of our town. You would never fit in. And I won't let you ruin our good name by you having an affair with him. You need someone like a hired hand. That' s good enough for you, if anybody will ever have you. Now go get me my milking sieve, and we'll milk the cows. Nightfall is coming."

Lilly did not cry. She knew what was going to happen. And she continued to carry food and drink to her suitor when he delivered the mail. It was during this time that he asked her to marry him.

She said, "Yes! Yes! Yes!"

Two black children on their way to church danced together and sang "Ezekiel Saw de Wheel", which made Bart and Lilly laugh. The children put their arms around each other's waists sang and danced in a folk-like manner to the song. Across the fields, a black church choir was singing the same song for Sunday Meeting. The cadence of the spiritual echoed the centuries of deep faith and commitment to

God that the Negro race had.

After a year Esther wanted to come home, and she met her brothers in Washington D.C., where they acted like laughing, giggling school children: visiting the Smithsonian Institute, the National Gallery of Art, the Capital Building, and the White House. They were so happy to be reunited that they could not wait to get home.

But for Lilly home became a type of hellish prison with no parole in sight. Nettie was working her doubly hard for Esther's return. Except for Esther's kindness, Lilly was not happy at staying with the Conways anymore. She wanted her own home.

As Esther's homecoming was approaching, Lilly's anticipation grew because the day Esther would come home; Lilly would elope with Bart that night.

Everyone could hardly wait until Esther arrived. She was to come (with her brothers) in on the morning train. Lilly wore her best dress. John Conway looked over the house as if appraising every fixture in detail. His daughter was the apple of his eye.

As the train pulled into the station, it seemed to let out a sigh of relief through the smoke.

"I'm so glad to be home!" Esther cried, as she hugged her mother then her father, and in turn, her brothers and Lilly. Lilly tried to hold her tears back because she knew her whole life would be changed before sunrise tomorrow.

The glazed ham, roast beef, fried chicken, corn-on-the-cob, black eyed peas, okra, rice, macaroni and cheese, cornbread biscuits, pickled peaches, homemade sweet bread and butter pickles, fresh apple pie, banana pudding, and peach cobbler were laid on the sideboard with clean starched linen napkins laid lightly over them to preserve them from flies. Large cold pitchers of buttermilk and sweet milk were brought from the ice house.

Esther smiled at all the food on the sideboard.
"No one can or preserve or pickle like my mother can," Esther said.

"I can," thought Lilly.

No one in the Conway household thought Lilly would amount to anything. Nettie had kept Lilly from going to school with Esther and the boys when basic skills were being taught. Esther was good about showing Lilly what she was learning, but Lilly was not availed with a trained teacher or classroom atmosphere.

That night after the festivities and everyone was asleep, Lilly met Bart Hadley behind the barn and they walked through the back forty together bathed in the limelight of a full moon. It puzzled her a little that she could smell liquor on his breath, but Lilly was too excited and happy to let anything worry her now. This was the first time that Lilly felt that she was a free woman. She had constructed many plans in her head. And somewhat like her mother before her, she thought that everything would fall into place. Bart seemed to really love her. He tended to be more quiet and serious than she was.

Sometimes moody and distant, he drank quite frequently. Lilly knew this, but she contented herself that he would change. She would change him. He came from one of the most prominent families in Citrus, Alabama. Lilly thought her days of housework would be altered to instructing the housemaids and kitchen maids on how to polish the silver and stir the gravy correctly. She knew how to run a good home. Nettie's scolding/teaching for the last twelve years was indelible.

I wonder what Nettie will say when she sees I'm gone and has to make breakfast for the family by herself, Lilly thought. A little smile of satisfaction played around her pink lips. Bart helped her through the last fence on the Conway farm and into a closed-in carriage. The wooden wheels were painted black and the seats were leather. An old man who had worked for the Hadley family for years took the reins as they got in and lightly tapped the horses on their backbones. This was a real adventure to Lilly, she almost felt like Cinderella. She thought every tale and every book on the subject of love could not be as good as this, though she really was a novice to love. The carriage slowed down and stopped at a white picket fence. There was a sign on the gate: "Will Conduct Marriages and/ or Funerals for Fee". The Old man stepped down from the carriage, and Bart held Lilly's hand as she stepped down. All three stood at the door in front of the house and waited for someone to open it. A middle aged woman appeared and led them into a parlor. The preacher said a few words and pronounced them man and wife. Lilly's head was a little dizzy with all the work she had done getting ready for Esther's homecoming and cleaning up all the dirty dishes and pots. As she kissed Bart she noticed that his breath smelled strong of alcohol that made her sick.

Another thirty miles and they had reached the hotel where they were to spend two weeks' honeymoon.

Lilly could not have been more exhausted. She took off her bonnet and dropped it in a large velvet chair. Her clothes felt like hot, binding fetters—layers of smothering cloth that stuck to her skin with acrid perspiration.

"I hope that I've done the right thing," she mused as she washed her face in a bowl of water. Bart did come from a wealthy family. One of his sisters, the oldest, was a school teacher. And his younger sister, Suzanna, was going to be married to a young accountant in the First Bank of Citrus, Alabama.

Lilly and Bart laughed under the covers on the first morning of their marriage. Lilly could not have been happier. She was going to be taken care of by her husband. And now, she could not express her joy. Nettie could not harm her. She was free at last. She wanted everybody to be as happy as she was. She wanted the whole world to feel her euphoria. Everything was good, nothing was bad. She lounged in a hot tub of water. She had never had such luxury, such total realization. Her eyes looked dreamily at the water as several bubbles floated on an upward course. The two weeks ended, and with tears in her eyes, Lilly put her foot up on the carriage, with Bart's hand under her elbow to boost her up.

"We'll go over to the General Store and get you some new clothes," said Bart.

Lilly chose three new dresses and Bart paid for them in cash. If this was what marriage was like, Lilly believed it was going to be fun.

As the carriage horses made their way back to Citrus, they seemed to know that they were on their way home. They seemed to pick up their hooves a little higher and arch their necks with dignity in anticipation.

The house on the Hadley Farm had a large porch veranda on three sides. A white scroll of wood curled around the comers of the eves as purple bougainvillea climbed up the white trellises and opened into sprays of wine-colored fans. There was no finer farm in the county, aside from the Conway Farm.

The sun was just rising as they rolled through the glare at full gallop. Bart made a sweeping gesture of a bow as two housemaids, his two sisters, and his ailing mother walked out on the back porch. Mama, Charlotte, and Suzanna put their hands on their hips. Their faces gave the impression of grinning Cheshire cats, but in reality they were false masks.

"Mama, and all I'd like you to meet my new bride."

"Wished you had married Esther instead," drawled Charlotte. "We would have had a big wedding for her with all our friends and all the trimmings."

"You all know Lilly, Mama?" Bart quizzed. He seemed oblivious to everything his sisters said.

"Why, yes," Mother Hadley said, "she makes the finest preserves in the county."

The two sisters were disappointed by Bart's choice, but as long as Mama seemed to approve of her, they had little else to say and walked back into the house.

Lilly was a little tired from the carriage ride. But when she smelled the ham and redeye gravy, hot biscuits and butter, and eggs frying on the grill, she got busy and helped the other girls serve breakfast. Lilly so wanted to make a good impression with Charlotte and Suzanna, but all she did was emphasize that her education was mainly in the kitchen. As she helped wash the breakfast dishes, dry them, and put them away, one of the sisters said: "Well, I've never washed a dish in my life. How shall we introduce her to our friends? What can she talk about?"

Lilly was worn out by now; more from how she was being treated than from working at chores she began to cry softly. She did not want Charlotte and Suzanna to hear her. One of the housemaids named Cassey, said, "Now, don't you pay them no mind Miss Lilly, you know more about running a house than all three of those women put together."

"I didn't have the chance to go to school much when I was young," said Lilly. "My mother made me stay at home and do the chores."

The other girl called Barbara said, "There's a teacher from the North, a Methodist Preacher, he teaches reading, writing, and arithmetic. All you have to do is ask Mr. Bart to pay a fee." This news was too good to be true for Lilly.

That evening she asked Bart if she could have the money for lessons. Bart saw the anticipation in Lilly's eyes. "I'll contact the teacher and give him money in advance," he said. "You can start as soon as possible."

Bart was only too happy to give Lilly an outlet. He would have more time to drink with his friends, and he could see that his sisters were not going to share their friendship so this might keep her from being lonely or depressed.

Next Saturday afternoon was Lilly's first appointment to be tutored. She had great expectations. The teacher, Reverend Edward Brock, was a quiet young man. Lilly began to learn very quickly from his teaching. His accent was different from what she was familiar with, but he was a very patient and kind teacher. Lilly began coming to Mr. Brock three, then four days a week, and Bart paid the fees. She excelled in all subjects which prompted Mr. Brock to begin teaching her history, classical poetry, and accounting. Lilly excelled in business subjects, yet she still loved English and poetry best.

Her reading greatly improved over the three months period that she had studied with Mr. Brock. Lilly was now three months pregnant with Bart's baby. Bart let her off at Edward's small frame house beside a narrow dirt road. The oak tree that stood by the house, spread its branches into large green canopies in varied directions as a shade from the sun. It was like a dream come true. All these years Lilly had wanted an education, and all these years Nettie had denied her this gift. The result was a hunger for the finer things an education could bring-fine clothes, music, paintings, furniture, the analysis of historic literature, and what was being written at present, and well-bred horses. Through Edward's eyes, Lilly saw life as it should be lived. A well-organized farm run like a company. The workers would be paid a salary and be given shares in the company according to the individual's work output. Bonuses and incentive would be given as productivity increased. Not only the owner, but also the worker would be afforded a very high standard of living. The worker might, in time think of the farm as his own.

These were the golden days of learning and leisure for Lilly, and she savored them as long as she could. She loved Edward from a platonic perspective. She had learned so much from him. There was a small voice in her head that seemed to tell her that her days with Edward's hand guiding her into the paths of the poets, and his methods of teaching from marketing to designing a first rate, well organized productive farm were numbered.

There had been whispers about this high thinker from the North, not respecting the culture of the South. And what were all the lights doing on in his house late in the evening? There were too many people congregating at his house at night.

Word got around that he was teaching Blacks at night. The Klu Klux Klan gave him a warning which Edward ignored. He was just to stick to teaching white children. As was his custom, Edward would let as many black adults and children as could fit in his house come to learn basic skills and upper levels. Some people sat on the floor while he expounded on the properties of addition, subtraction, multiplication, and division. Night after night, Edward would go over what they had gone over the night before; and then he began to cover new territory. The training was becoming noticeable. A black farmer would have been cheated nearly $1,000.00 in buying a parcel of land adjacent to his land because the seller added a $1,000.00 to the agreed price. Ross Haze caught the discrepancy and would not budge until the infraction was reviewed and corrected by a lawyer. Lilly was practically oblivious to what was going on and Bart was beginning to enjoy their conversations at night while they lay in bed.

It was early Saturday morning and Lilly was about to embark onto the winding foothills of Citrus, Alabama, the home of Edward Brock. Edward was going to test her to see if she was ready to receive her high school diploma. She was so excited that she could hardly contain herself. Bart seemed to take much pleasure in her excitement. As the carriage started to roll, Charlotte came out on the veranda.

"Better say goodbye to your teacher," she said.

Lilly looked back, but Charlotte talked in such depressed trite undertones that Lilly tried not to pay much attention to her.

Edward greeted both Lilly and Bart. He was glad that Bart had a degree of open-mindedness as Lilly was very gifted.

Lilly took the four tests and finished with a half hour to spare. Edward promised to mail the test for certification in town that evening. Lilly embraced Edward, and he kissed her hand. "You're one of my prize students," he said. "I feel very grateful to have known you."

Lilly blushed, smiled, and looked down at her feet. "Words cannot express how much I appreciate you, Edward." Bart shook Edward's hand, and Lilly and Bart went home.

That evening Edward walked to town and posted Lilly's test. As he came down the steps of the post office, a person with a pointed hood and white robe rode up the steps on horseback. Another person helped the first rider encircle Edward Brock. Torch lights could be seen from every direction of town. How the Klu Klux Klan found out that Edward Brock was teaching black people basic skills at night, no one will ever know.

But whether there was a law written or unwritten, teaching blacks was not welcomed in the deep South.

The white robes made a sharp contrast with the blackness of the night. The fear aroused by those white robes and hoods was as contagious as if a plague had entered the town. Such fear might have generated enough electricity to light the whole town square and many blocks more.

As twenty robed men rode up, Edward was totally surrounded. "Gentlemen, what are you going to do?" Edward asked. A noose was thrown over Edward's neck. "In the eyes of both God and man, you are in the wrong and you will have to answer for it." Edward said.

There was very little ceremony. The other end of the rope was thrown over a hinge which jutted out from the post office building. It did not take much effort to hang Edward. No pleading for his case would have changed the verdict. Teaching Negroes was a crime in Alabama, as in many Southern states in 1884, and the Klu Klux Klan was used as an arm to enforce it.

Klansmen had been rounding up "would-be" scholars, who were walking to Edward's house, taking their books from them. They enjoyed showing off their horsemanship, forcing students—young and old—to relinquish their books. They were proud of their rule over these people.

A cross was erected and set on fire. The books which the Klansmen had brought from Edward Brock's house was thrown on the flames which intensified their fury. The faces of the students, both young and old, showed despair. Some of the women began to weep and this started a floodgate of tears from children who were already terrified.

There was no human authority figure, no policeman to protect the black community. Some of the children had managed to get away and were hiding in the woods. Some of the children had run to the church to try to find the preacher, but he was out of town. With what few books they had carried away, they hid in the church. There was a fear that the Klu Klux Klan would burn the church down. Many prayers were being prayed in undertones.

None of the Klansmen said very much, they nodded to each other and made signs and gestures with their hands to keep anyone from recognizing them. It was as if the following events had been deliberately rehearsed with great conviction.

A black woman in her thirties had been making her way to Edward Brock's house when she saw the robed men, she hid in an abandoned building near the post office, thinking that the men would soon go away. A Klansman, who was on foot, found her and forced her out the front door. She was holding several textbooks in her hands and the Klansman ordered her to toss them into the fire. These were the first books that she had ever held or opened, and she never wanted to part with them. When she would not obey, the Klansman, slapped her across the face, grabbed the books and tossed them in the fire.

Even though the woman feared the man greatly, with all her reserves of strength, she lunged toward the fire to retrieve the books. The fire that curled the pages burned her hands as she cried out in pain. A rope was thrown around her, and she was dragged by a white-robed horseman into the woods. The man got off his horse and dragged her to him.

She then drew back an arm and with all her might, socked him in the face. Recovering himself, the man spoke, "Why you!" His voice sounded familiar to her as he returned her blow. She lay unconscious. He looked at her helpless body on the ground and he slowly knelt by her, chuckled and started unbuttoning her dress. From the woods behind the man, two black teenage children, a boy and a girl, slowly and silently came up to the robed man and struck him with heavy oak branches that they used like clubs. They revived the woman, helped her to her feet, then all three vanished into the woods.

It was a still morning in the month of May when the bright sunshine showed the smoke rising from the embers of a once burning cross and as the smoke rose it loomed over the roof of the post office.

Lilly blinked her eyes, rubbed her head and yawned. She could not understand why it was so quiet at the Hadley home so late in the morning. She turned over in bed to see if she could hear Cassey and Barbara in the kitchen, either washing breakfast dishes or frying bacon. "Where is everybody?" Lilly thought. She had slept late that morning because she had had nightmares and did not get much sleep. Bart had already dressed and gone. As she made her way slowly to a pitcher and bowl, she poured the cold water over her hands. She washed her face and neck. The sun was getting brighter and Lilly squinted as she tried to look for a familiar person in the yard. "Something was wrong," she thought. She found a clean dress and tried to button it down the back by herself. Frustrated with the buttons, she began to call for Cassey and Barbara. She heard quick steps from the kitchen, and Barbara came into the room. She wasted no time in telling Lilly the bad news.

"Mr. Brock dead," Barbara said quickly. "He hanging from the eaves of the post office. Klu Klux Klan killed him." The shock was almost too much for Lilly. She was eight months pregnant and close to having her baby.

Lilly's mind went back to all the wonderful learning experiences that only Edward and she had enjoyed. She remembered sitting in front of a roaring fire in the dead of winter, reading Keats, Browning, Thoreau, and Shelly. She recalled portions of sonnets from Shakespeare. Life had been more palatable, and not as foreboding. Life had been safe as long as Lilly could escape the mundane through Edward's creative mind. And now that mind was gone. His voice and personality were gone forever.

Lilly had the horses harnessed by the stablemen and clicked the reins on the horses lightly as she drove them out of the stable. Tears were streaming down her face, and she made great gulping sounds as she drove the horses closer to town she wished Bart had been there to comfort her. There was stillness in the air that she had never noticed before, an eerie atmosphere prevailed on what should have been a perfectly beautiful spring day.

The buildings were coming closer to Lilly. Her head ached as the horses galloped past the first buildings. At last her wagon stopped in front of the body of the man who had been her teacher, friend, confidant, and mentor. She jumped down from the wagon and tried to pull the rope which held the noose in tack. Again and again, she pulled and tugged on the rope without success.

"Will somebody help me, please?" Lilly pleaded. As she looked around, she noticed that there was neither man nor beast near the body of Edward Brock.

"Somebody! Please help me! Please help me, somebody!"

Seemingly out of nowhere stepped two black men. As one man held Edward's body to keep it from falling to the ground, the other, who was carrying a knife, cut the rope. Both men gathered the body in their arms and carried it to Lilly's wagon. Lilly got in the seat, and the two men sat in the back with the body. Scores of black women, men and children came out of hiding and walked along the sides of the wagon. A valuable friend had been lost and there would be much grieving by many people. A man on horseback slowly walked in front of the wagon to lead the way. Near the black burial ground, the man and horse turned in and went to a place near a large oak tree. Several men had brought shovels and picks. A grave was being dug for Edward Brock. As four or five men broke the sod, many other people broke out in singing well-known Negro Spirituals: "Swing Low Sweet Chariot", "Oh, When the Saints Go Marching In", "I Want Jesus to Walk With Me."

Myriads of black children ran through the fields, picking wild flowers for Edward's grave. A black preacher began to speak, and the crowd hushed as the body was wrapped and placed into the grave. The preacher stood over the grave and said, "Jesus said, 'Let not your heart be troubled: ye believe in God. Believe also in Me. In My Father's house are many mansions: if it were not so, I would have told you. I go to prepare a place for you. And if I go and prepare a place for you, I will come again and receive you unto Myself; that where I am, there you will be also. And wither I go you know, and the way you know.' Thomas, a disciple of Jesus, saith unto 'Him, Lord, we know not whither Thou goest; and how can we know the way?' Jesus saith unto him, 'I am the way, the truth and the life no man cometh unto the Father, but by Me. If ye had known Me, you should know My Father also; and from henceforth ye know Him, and have seen Him.'

Philip saith unto Him, 'Lord show us the Father, and it sufficeth us.' Jesus saith unto Him, 'Have I been so long time with you and yet hast thou not known Me, Philip? He that hath seen Me hath seen the Father, and how sayest thou then, show us the Father? Believest thou not that I am in the Father, and the Father in Me? The words that I speak unto you I speak not of Myself, but the Father that dwelleth in Me, He doth the works.

Believe Me that I am in the Father and the Father in Me, or else believe Me for the very work's sake. I will not leave you comfortless I will come to you. Yet a little while, and the world seeth Me no more; but ye shall see Me, because I live, ye shall live also.'

Amen."

The crowd began to disburse. Lilly threw herself on the grave and wept bitterly.

The preacher tried to do what he could for her. "You're going to have to let him go, Miss Lilly, he wouldn't want you cryin' like this."

Lilly got up; the preacher gave her his handkerchief to wipe her face. Lilly felt comforted by the old man.

"I don't understand why he had to die." She said. "He was always trying to do good."

"Maybe that why he had to die," the preacher said.

"I feel so tired," Lilly said.

"Guess it's about time for us to go home," the preacher said. "Let not your heart be troubled, Miss Lilly, neither let it be afraid," the preacher said, as he slowly walked down the road to his home.

The horses were sniffing at the grave. Flowers of every color were spread on top of the grave like a blanket. The shadows were forming along the surrounding hillsides, in about an hour the sun would set and darkness would cover

Edward's grave and all of Citrus, Alabama. Lilly got into the wagon; the wheels made loud creaking sounds as they matched the ruts in the orange colored clay road. Lilly's head ached and she began to have slight cramps in her stomach. She had been grieving so much for Edward that she had practically forgotten the new life within her. As she entered the Hadley farm, she felt fear well up inside of her. The lights were dim in the house, and no one was walking around the grounds. It was unusual to see the house so quiet.

Lilly left the horses standing in harness in the stable yard and crept up the back steps on the veranda that led to the kitchen. Barbara and Cassey were speaking in tones which were very hard to hear. Lilly appeared in the dim light for some hot tea. She had not eaten all day and felt very weak.

"Miss Lilly, we're glad you're here!" said both women at once.

"Miss Charlotte stirr'en up Mr. Bart to kick you off the place."

"Suzanna just cryin' and sayin' she gonna die!"

Lilly thought for a moment. "Barbara, you know where the Conway farm is? Go tell Miss Esther what is happening here, and tell her I'm not well. The horses are still harnessed in the stable yard."

"Yes, Miss Lilly, I'll go right away." Barbara hurried towards the stable yard.

Lilly went upstairs, took off her dress and went to bed in her underclothing. She was too tired to cry or be afraid, but she was concerned for her little one to be and her heavily fatigued body. She cared for Bart, but she knew that she did not belong as a family member on the Hadley Estate.

She longed to be free from so many voices, especially from Charlotte and Suzanna. To Lilly, Charlotte and Suzanna were no better than Nettie had been when she was a child. Bart tried to play down their cruelty, but Lilly stayed away from them as much as possible.

Lilly lit an oil lamp in her bedroom and tried to wipe away the tears from her face. "I feel dirty," she thought. "Oh, how I would love a hot tub bath! I wish I were on my honeymoon again. I could ring for the porter and he would order two or three waiters to pour steaming hot water in a tub anytime I wanted it." Lilly could almost feel the steam.

She had had little time to dream, little time to remember the days when she and Bart had courted by the Conway mailbox. She and Bart had made love and had loved each other on their honeymoon. Now her bed was cold, and the warm body of her husband was absent from the covers. He seemed distant and hard to reach. His drinking bouts were more and more frequent, and often he would not talk to her for days. The close rapport they had shared, talking of having a big farm someday, a general store, and deciding on how many children they would like to have seemed dreadfully out of reach. Their love had cooled and trust could be turned on and off like a faucet. A feeling of desperation caused Lilly to sink in an abyss of fear of the future and of fear of the unknown, causing her great fatigue. She seemed powerless to take control of her life. Suzanna partly created this atmosphere in observing Lilly closely and pointing out a barrage of bad habits that she had to Bart. "Where is my life going?" Lilly wondered.

As Lilly pondered on these things, Barbara was wrestling with the horses. They did not want to leave the stable yard. They had not been fed and had little rest since late morning. After playing tug of war with the horse's reins to get them to turn around; they finally gave in and turned around and bolted into the twilight. The dirt road looked narrower at night for there were no street lights. The serpentine turns around picturesque green foothills gave Citrus the demeanor of little change. Dim lights from tiny farms looked bright against the vast darkness of the woods.

Esther Conway was not married nor did not want to be. She felt that she was happy being single. Her life was comparatively full and her days unencumbered, until the right man came along. Esther was an accomplished artist and she wrote human interest stories for: *The Citrus Reporter* and also taught English in the Citrus Grammar School. Esther had just come home from her job at the small newspaper office and retired to the drawing room.

Barbara entered the Conway farm and asked one of the barn attendants to feed and water the horses. Then Barbara met a maid at the kitchen door and followed her into the house. The maid went into the drawing room and whispered to Esther to come with her.

Esther got up and came into the kitchen. Barbara told Esther that Lilly was having trouble with Charlotte and Suzanna and that Lilly wanted Esther to come and help calm them down. Esther quietly got her cape and bonnet and followed Barbara into the barn yard. Both women lighted into the wagon quickly and Barbara touched the backs of the horses lightly with the reins. Esther was sad to hear that

Lilly was being treated so badly by Charlotte and Suzanna. She was sad the Edward Brock had been killed. It seemed to her that life could be lived so simply and yet most people lived their lives under a spate of stressful episodes from people who could have been loving and supportive. There was destructive syndrome within the Hadley clan, much like the negative syndrome that Lilly had received from Nettie. Barbara re-rounded the roads that ribboned the foot hills of Citrus. It was about 7:30 P.M. when Barbara and Esther entered the Hadley driveway which curved around the house in the direction of the barn. Charlotte and Suzanna came out to greet Esther with hugs and kisses.

"We wish you were here instead of that trouble maker, Lilly," Charlotte complained.

"Yes, Esther, I just can't stand Lilly," Suzanna said.

Bart did not say a word.

Lilly had been standing just outside the room where everyone was talking and heard everything; she could take no more. She ran out the back porch stairs where the horses stood with feedbags on their heads.

"Take the feed away!" Lilly shouted to one of the hands. She mounted the wheel to position herself on the wagon seat. With reins in hand as they slipped the feedbags off the horses, she lashed the leather straps over the backs on the tired animals.

"Ha!" Lilly yelled, as Bart quickly bolted down the steps toward the wagon. He yelled for Lilly to stop, but she kept right on going. After they had gone down the road a far piece she slowed the horses down and drew a deep breath. She was glad to be away from people for awhile. On and on Lilly drove the horses until she turned off on a very narrow dirt road. She began to wonder how she was going to turn around. The unseen crickets were chirping loudly. Lilly saw what looked like birds come at her from many directions.

"It must be bats," she thought, as twilight turned into nightfall. The bats darted from one place to another, barely missing her it seemed. As her wagon created ruts in the salmon-colored clay which became softer and softer. Lilly found herself to be stuck on this lonesome side road in a part of suburban Citrus which she did not know. She had cooled off now and wished she had not been so hasty to run off from home especially on this night. She began to hear faint phrases of people's singing. The horses could go no further. They were slobbering from their mouths and now gasping for breath. Lilly could do nothing for them by herself, so she got down from the wagon and started walking toward the music. Lilly walked about a half mile. The moon was not very bright, and she half wondered to herself if she might have her baby right on this dirt road.

"Oh, I feel so tired," she thought to herself. "Why can't life be easier than this? Why can't things just fall into place? I wish Bart and I had our own farm, then I could choose the people I wanted to be near." As she rounded a curve, she saw lights a short distance away, "Thank God!" She thought.

People were sitting in pews and a young preacher got up to speak: "Let not your hearts be troubled. Ye believe in God, believe in also in Me. In my Father's house are many mansions; if it were not so, I would have told you. I go to prepare a place for you. And if I go and prepare a place for you, I will come again, and receive you unto Myself; that where I am, there ye may be also."

"People, that if thou shalt confess with thy mouth the Lord Jesus, and shalt believe in thine heart that God hath raised Him from the dead, thou shalt be saved. For with the heart man beleiveth unto righteousness; and with the mouth confession is made unto salvation."

"For the scripture saith, 'Who so ever beleiveth on Him shall not be ashamed. For there is no difference between the Jew and the Greek.' For the same Lord overall is rich unto all that call upon Him."

The choir began to sing: "Just as I Am". Lilly had heard the young preacher say some of the words that the elderly black preacher had spoken during Edward's funeral.

The preacher spoke again, "Anyone who will repent, be sorry for their sins, and ask Jesus into his or her heart as their personal Saviour will gain heaven if they truly believe."

Again the choir sang another chorus of "Just As I Am". Lilly began to walk forward with the rest of the people moving from the congregation to the front of the altar. She knelt at the bench.

An older woman came to her and knelt by her side. "Will you accept Jesus as your personal Saviour?"

Lilly said, "Yes."

"Then let' s say the sinner's prayer together," the older woman said.

"Dear Lord Jesus, I am sorry for my sins," Lilly prayed. "And dear Lord, please come into my heart and be my Saviour in Jesus' Name. Amen."

"You will never be sorry you prayed that prayer." said the woman.

"What is your name daughter?"

"Lilly Conway Hadley." Lilly said as she wiped a tear away.

The woman smiled a broad smile, and wiped a tear away on her own face. "Lilly! I'm your mother!" Bonnie said.

Tears were streaming down both of their faces. It was a time of rebirth and a promising future.

"I never thought that I would ever meet you or be able to speak to you ever!" Lilly cried. Nettie had drilled it into her head that she was a Conway, and that she had no other relatives. But Lilly could remember the very pretty, sweet blonde lady who had tried to take her away when she was a little girl, and Nettie had taken a rug batting stick and had beaten her away. She remembered the cries of the young girl and the loneliness when she was gone. The hatred of Nettie and her children's attitude not caring for Lilly one way or the other except for Esther was a scenario void of love Esther had saved her from feelings of the total depravity of love. And now Bonnie had saved her from the same feelings coming from Charlotte and Suzanna. I tried to take you away long ago but Mrs. Conway would not let me. I wanted to keep you, but my father gave you to John Conway. John Conway was rich and the law was on his side. Both women got up from the mourners' bench and embraced each other. As they walked down the narrow isle to the back of the church, Lilly felt warm water flowing down her legs.

"I think my baby's going to be born now," she sighed.

Some of the men in the congregation freed Lilly's wagon from the soft sand and the two women drove the horses slowly to Bonnie's home. Bonnie put her shawl around Lilly to warm her. The narrow road wound deep into the woods. The voices of the crickets and the dim on-and-off lights of the fireflies kept the travelers' company. Lilly looked very pale.

"I'll give you some warm milk and molasses to give you some strength," Bonnie said.

The owls lighted from tree to tree looking for the slightest sound of mouse or vermin.

"I don't think I can stand the pain much longer," Lilly grimaced.

"It's not much farther daughter," Bonnie said quietly.

A small shack stood in a clearing in the woods. Even though it had bare floors and too few pieces of furniture, it was clean and cozy. A sight that pleased Lilly for she was close to delivery. It was about 4:30 A.M. when the first new cries of Ben Hadley penetrated the quiet atmosphere of the dense woods. The air was permeated with the smell of bacon, fried eggs, and cat's head biscuits. Fresh butter was laid on the table, and the scent of pine and wildflowers came into the house via hundreds of acres of woods.

Lilly had been oblivious of any people in the house when she was helped onto a bed. Clean sheets and quilts covered the bed that she lay on. After the birth, Lily slept for a long time. Her face was bloated and pale and she was very weak. Her labor had been hard. About 2:00 P.M. Lilly woke up. She was hungry. She dreamt a great portion of the morning. In the dream she was driving a wagon on a narrow road during a mist. She could not see very far before her nor could she see very far on the sides, and she could see nothing behind. She felt that she was completely at the mercy of the whim of the horses and of the mists and of the miles and miles of salmon colored sod that threaded through uncharted woods of what seemed to be her destiny. The mists were types of curtains which prevented her from seeing too far. Yet, the horses galloped on methodically, as though they knew the terrain and had travelled over the road many times. Totally oblivious to any pull she made on the reins. Lilly took a deep breath and tried to train her mind on her new baby. "He is beautiful, isn't he, Mother?" Lilly asked.

"He sure is, honey." Bonnie said.

Bonnie had married Percy Cole two years after she was separated from Lilly. And in the following years she had borne Percy five girls and two boys. The harshness of the years had left her face worn, and although she was still a handsome woman, the striking beauty that she had held John Conway with years ago had dissipated. Her body had grown larger through childbearing, and there were deep lines under her beautiful violet eyes. Percy had done what he could for her, but he was Unlearned and very poor. He worked in a sap mill in the nearby town of Cartersville, Alabama.

"I had five more girls," Bonnie said with tears in her eyes, "But no one could take the place of my Lilly."

Ben began to cry with muted sounds as Bonnie put him in Lilly' s arms she drew a deep sigh. "I sent Percy to tell Mr. Bart that you' re here," Bonnie said.

"I'm glad you did," said Lilly. "He's probably worried sick, if not about me, then about the baby."

"Oh, Honey, I'm sure he is very worried about you too!" Bonnie cried.

A blast of noise started coming up the road. Horses and carriages circled around the back and sides of the house, and six men two by two stepped in a cadence up the front porch steps, but there was one hard knock at the door. "1 would like to see my wife, Lilly," Bart Hadley said, with a deep southern drawl.

"Come right on in," Bonnie said. "She's in the front bedroom."

Bart entered the room and shut the door. He moved quietly over to Lilly's bed.

"Sugar, I'm sorry for the way I acted toward you, it will never happen again."

Lilly turned toward him. "Bart, most of it was my fault. Right now I just don't fit in with your world. I guess it was the way I was treated when I was growing up. The Conways, especially Nettie, treated me as a slave more than a member of the family. I need a family, Bart, and I need a good friend."

"You have a family, Lilly, and you have a friend."

"Oh, Bart, I love you so," said Lilly.

They kissed each other. "We're not really good enough for you." Bart said.

"Lilly, I've decided to move us to Texas, so you won't be bothered by my sisters again." Lilly showed sudden extreme happiness. Her smile seemed radiant. For the first time she felt that she had a handle on her own destiny.

Bart gently picked up Ben and cradled him in his arms. "I am a father now and I will try to take it seriously. And I will try to love my wife better," he said. Everything seemed to be falling into place. It was all too good to be true. Getting ready to go back to the Hadley Farm was not a problem for Lilly because she knew she wouldn't be there for long. In a few days they would be on their way to Austin, Texas.

Lilly kissed Bonnie and her half-sisters and brothers and got into the buckboard with the baby.

"Take good care of your sweet self, Honey," Bonnie said. "I love you."

Love is such a small word, but it means so much, Lilly thought. I'm going to say it to Ben and Bart always. As she thought this, the wagon rolled off slowly, and they were on their way home.

Spring was drawing off into summer. The day was warm and the sun seemed to wrap itself around her with a penetrating warmth. Lilly pulled Ben's blanket over his eyes to protect him from the bright glare. She had such great expectations.

Everything was perfect now: she had her baby, her husband was back, and she had met and loved her real mother and her real mother loved her. She was leaving Bart's family home for hopefully greener pastures. The wagon turned and twisted in and out of the woodlands; and then moved into cleared fields, cotton and tobacco and corn. Finally, they rolled onto Hadley land. The dogwoods and magnolias shaded the bulk of the passengers as they finally came to a stop in front of the grand old house. The two sisters and another woman came out on the front porch. The other woman was Nettie.

"I wish you had died in childbirth!" Nettie said. "You've killed my Esther!"

"I, what?" Shouted Lilly. "I did no such thing!"

"You sent for her, and now she's dying!" Nettie shouted back.

"Where is she?" asked Lilly.

"Conway land, Missy."

Lilly asked Bart to take her there, and off they went. Later it was found out that one of the cows on the Conway farm had TB, but Nettie wanted to dig her claws in for the last time.

Lilly suddenly became nauseated and very tired again. Esther had been her friend and her mother when she was growing up. She had kept Nettie from totally terrorizing her from the time she was four years old. And now her old friend and mentor was mortally ill.

When Lilly got to Esther's bedside, Esther was coughing up blood. "You didn't' t do this," Esther sighed. "Don't let Mama buffalo you again. I'm going to Arizona in the morning to try to get cured."

"I'll miss you baby," Esther said. "I always thought of you as my baby," Esther tried to smile.

Lilly started crying, "You've always been there for me. I don't know what I'll do without you, Esther, you've been like a mother to me, and my best friend."

"You'll go on living, no matter what happens," Esther said. "You' re a smart girl. Take good care of your sweet self. You have a new baby. I don't want you to catch this stuff. Goodbye, I love you."

Lilly kissed her forehead and left the room. It seemed a bridge from the past was burning irreversibly. She again was not sure of the future; but with the assurance of a new spirit springing up within her, she was not alone. No matter what happened in her life in the future, she knew that God would be with her. Her decision to take Jesus into her heart a few hours ago had generated a knowledge of God that she had never known.

That night, Lilly could not sleep. The baby could feel her unrest, and he cried intermittently throughout the night. Lilly rocked him and cradled him mechanically, but her thoughts were for Esther. She did not want Esther to die, and yet there was no cure for TB. Tomorrow they would be on their way to Austin, Texas, and Esther would be on a train to Arizona.

"Oh God, help me," Lilly said.

A breeze seemed to whisper, "I will never leave thee nor forsake thee."

Lilly felt that God was now directing her life. She could be at peace and concentrate on her family. She had been concentrating on herself instead of her home or her husband. She decided to remedy the situation. For a start, Bart would take Lilly and Ben to Texas where they would be a family, and God willing have a bigger family, and Lilly would be running the household. A smile came to Lilly's face as she entertained this thought as she drifted off to sleep.

The morning seemed to come too soon and emptied into several hours of backbreaking work. Four wagons were filled to the brim with commodities: clothing, food, furniture, and medical supplies. The garbled whines of the sisters' goodbyes was a last tribute to the validity of their reason for the move. Smiles of a masked nature, as if they were painted on, were engraved on the young couples' faces.

The wind picked up the sand in the dry grass and started flurries like tiny tornadoes whirling around in the air. The wagons started forward and the Hadley gate was left behind in the distance as if it were a thing of the past. Lilly made a sigh of great relief. For the first time, she was the master of her own household, and it felt good. She was free from the criticisms of another woman making her feel that she was not good enough.

The wagon rambled on and she nursed her baby in a peaceful atmosphere, conscious of the baby's sucking sounds and Bart's steady hands on the reins as he clapped them from time to time on the horses' backs.

They were headed due southwest to Austin, the capital of Texas. Bart had some friends out there, and he meant to strike it rich. Bart had invested $2,000.00 in the wild cat oil business, and he also wanted to try running horses. He received word that one oil well had already hit oil. They were expecting other wells to gush in a few months.

Lilly really didn't care where they were headed as long as they were headed away from Citrus, Alabama. The contrasts of the terrain was evident after the first hundred miles. The foothills began to flatten into plains. The baby was asleep inside the wagon and Bart and Lilly sat in front. This was the third evening on the road. Lilly took a deep breath.

"I love you, Honey," Lilly said.

"I love you too, baby." Bart said.

He put his arm around her. The stars were coming out and darkness seemed to be absorbing the existing light.

"We'll make camp pretty soon," Bart said.

They came to what looked like to be a good place to camp and placed the wagons in a box like circle. The men in the other wagons got down and made camp. The meat was started on a large grill, and the beans quickly followed. Two kettles of hot water were set on the fire for coffee and biscuit dough was being kneaded for cat's head biscuits where blackstrap molasses would be used to sop the biscuits, a meal that would stick to their ribs and keep them going.

Lilly, now was very grateful to Nettie, in that she had been married a little over a year and was able to take care of a household. She was not grateful for the way she had been taught, but her biscuits were as light as Nettie's. As she sat gazing into the campfire, Lilly thought about the Conway home. It seemed more than just a year and a half that she and Bart walked across the Conway fields and got married. Then she thought about her mother, Bonnie. Bonnie had been so beautiful as a young girl. Now, she was faded, and old even though in years she was still quite a young woman. Poverty and a hard life did not spare her beauty. She had had many children. It seemed she was destined to live out her life in obscurity and impoverishment. All this could not diminish the joy they both had when she lead Lilly to Jesus Christ. This was a bond that could never be broken for all eternity.

Ben was lying on Lilly's lap as the fire was heaped with logs. Everything was peaceful and serene, a very pleasant setting to remember the past by.

Bart leaned over and said gently, "Honey, you're almost asleep. Let me take Ben and both of you can go to sleep in the wagon."

Lilly yawned and got in the wagon.

Their wagon rolled into Austin in the early afternoon. It was a turning point for the Hadley family.

As the months went by, Lilly became pregnant again. She remembered the pain and discomfort that she had had with Ben and yet she looked forward to a little girl.

She would name her after Lilly's mother, Bonnie Margaret, and Esther. Her baby's name would be Margaret Esther. She thought this would make up for the friendships that she had missed out on most of her childhood and most of her married life.

They bought a two-story house just outside of Austin. Ben was now about a year old and Margaret Esther had just been born.

"Isn't she beautiful?" Lilly said.

"Honey, she is the picture of your mother, a blue-eyed blond.,

"I hoped that she would look like her, Bart, they're going to say someday, there's nobody prettier than a Hadley girl.,

"Yes, Honey, you're sure right about that. Nobody has prettier blue eyes or blonde hair."

"Can we have more, Bart?"

"Honey, with the oil wells coming in as they are and the sale of the horses, we'll have as many as we want."

Lilly contented herself that she was starting a generation of females and males, her offspring would be good Christian boys and girls. She would show them how to do things and would teach them how to find good wives and good husbands. Being well-to-do would not hurt her offspring either. She promised herself that she would manage money the way Edward had taught her.

In fact, in the course of time, they would have eight children. Each child was special to Lilly and as each child was born, she poured out to them as much love as she knew how to give. She tried to give what Esther and Edward had given to her. A mixture of respect and fairness. She gave them as much attention as she could equally with kindness and a gentle spirit. And in doing this she seemed to see herself as now satisfied with life and at peace.

* * *

www.ingramcontent.com/pod-product-compliance
Lightning Source LLC
Chambersburg PA
CBHW030023060826
49398CB00031B/204

* 9 7 9 8 8 9 3 8 9 0 5 5 6 *